A Crabby Book

Get Well, Crabby!

ACORN™
SCHOLASTIC INC.

Jonathan
Fenske

To Jen and Eric, doctors of medicine **and** friendship!

Library of Congress Cataloging-in-Publication Data

Names: Fenske, Jonathan, author, illustrator.

Title: Get well, Crabby! / Jonathan Fenske.

Description: First edition. | New York : Acorn/Scholastic Inc, 2022. |

Series: A Crabby book ; 4

Summary: When Crabby gets sick, Plankton is determined to play doctor and take care of his friend, even if Crabby does not want the help—until Crabby realizes that he can get Plankton to do all of his household chores.

Identifiers: LCCN 2021022307 | ISBN 9781338767827 (paperback) | ISBN 9781338767834 (hardback)

Subjects: LCSH: Crabs—Juvenile fiction. | Plankton—Juvenile fiction. | Friendship—Juvenile fiction. | Conduct of life—Juvenile fiction. | Humorous stories. | CYAC: Crabs—Fiction. | Plankton—Fiction. | Sick—Fiction. | Friendship—Fiction. | Humorous stories. | BISAC: JUVENILE FICTION / Readers / Beginner | JUVENILE FICTION / Social Themes / Friendship | LCGFT: Humorous fiction.

Classification: LCC PZ7.F34843 Ge 2022 | DDC (E)—dc23

LC record available at https://lccn.loc.gov/2021022307

10 9 8 7 6 5 4 3 2 1   22 23 24 25 26

Printed in China   62

First edition, January 2022
Edited by Katie Heit
Book design by Maria Mercado

2

3

4

YES! I am sure I am not—AA—

AA—

AAA—

ACHOO!

5

Yep. You are sick.

SNIFF SNIFF

Fine. I am sick.

Do not worry, Crabby! I will take care of you!

How will **you** take care of me? You are not a **nurse**.

7

Plankton, you are not a nurse. You are also not a **doctor**.

Oh, yes, I am! I went to Friendship School!

Doctors do not go to **Friendship** School! Doctors go to **Medical** School.

Wait right there!

9

THE FEVER

13

Great idea!

Now hold it for ten seconds!

YANK!

17

THE BANDAGE

This bandage should fix you up, Crabby!

A bandage? I do not need a bandage.

SNIFF
SNIFF

23

But I **really** want to use my bandage.

Look! It is a **mostly clean** bandage.

Mostly clean?

Please?

27

33

THE CURE

You are sick, Crabby. And the cure is **rest**!

It is just the **sniffles**. I do not need rest.

SNIFF
SNIFF

37

39

41

43

44

About the Author

Jonathan Fenske lives in South Carolina with his family. He was born in Florida near the ocean, so he knows all about life at the beach! He thinks the worst part about being sick is having to miss playtime!

Jonathan is the author and illustrator of several children's books including **Barnacle Is Bored**, **Plankton Is Pushy** (a Junior Library Guild selection), and **After Squidnight** (an Indie Next Pick). His early reader **A Pig, a Fox, and a Box** was a Theodor Seuss Geisel Honor Book.

THESE BOOKS ARE NOT FUNNY.

Barnacle Is BORED
Jonathan Fenske

Plankton Is PUSHY
Jonathan Fenske

YOU CAN DRAW CLAMMY!

I'm as happy as a clam!

1. Draw a football shape.

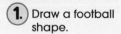

2. Make one long squiggly line and one small curved line for the mouth.

3. Add two circles for eyes.

4. Give Clammy an expression by adding lines and dots to the eyes.

5. Color Clammy with your favorite colors!

6. Add some fun details for decoration!

WHAT'S YOUR STORY?

Crabby is sick! Plankton tries to help Crabby feel better.
How would **you** try to help Crabby feel better?
Would Plankton and Clammy help you take care of Crabby?
Write and draw your story!